One morning, the bears went out for a walk. A few minutes later, a little girl came along. Her name was Goldilocks, because she had bright yellow hair. When she saw that the cottage door was not quite closed, she pushed it open and went inside!

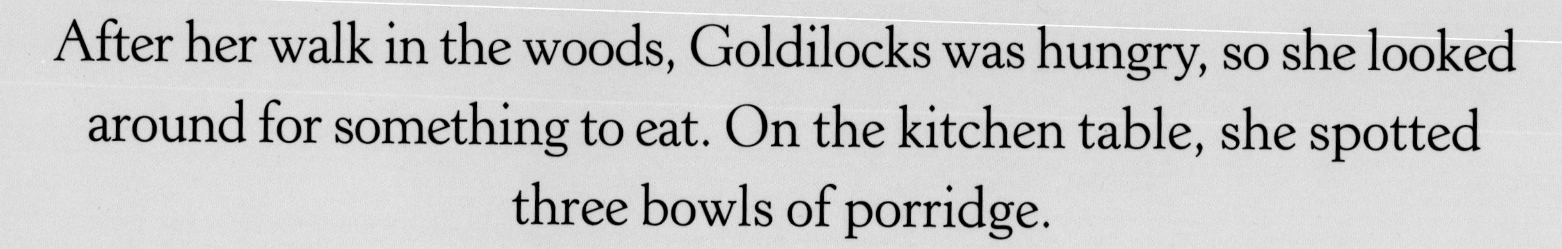

After her walk in the woods, Goldilocks was hungry, so she looked around for something to eat. On the kitchen table, she spotted three bowls of porridge.

She went straight to the biggest bowl, picked up Father Bear's large spoon, and took a mouthful. "Ouch!" cried Goldilocks. "Much too hot!"

She picked up Mother Bear's medium-sized spoon
and tasted *her* porridge.
"*Eeeeeeuuuuw!* Much too sweet!" she said.

Last of all, she tried Baby Bear's porridge.
Now Goldilocks didn't say a word. She was much too busy eating!

When she was full, Goldilocks wandered into the living room. She saw three chairs – one large, one medium-sized and one tiny. Goldilocks climbed on to the huge armchair in the corner.

Ow! It was much too hard.

She leapt down and went over to the middle-sized chair. Goldilocks hauled herself up and nearly disappeared! The chair was so soft, she almost sank beneath the cushions.

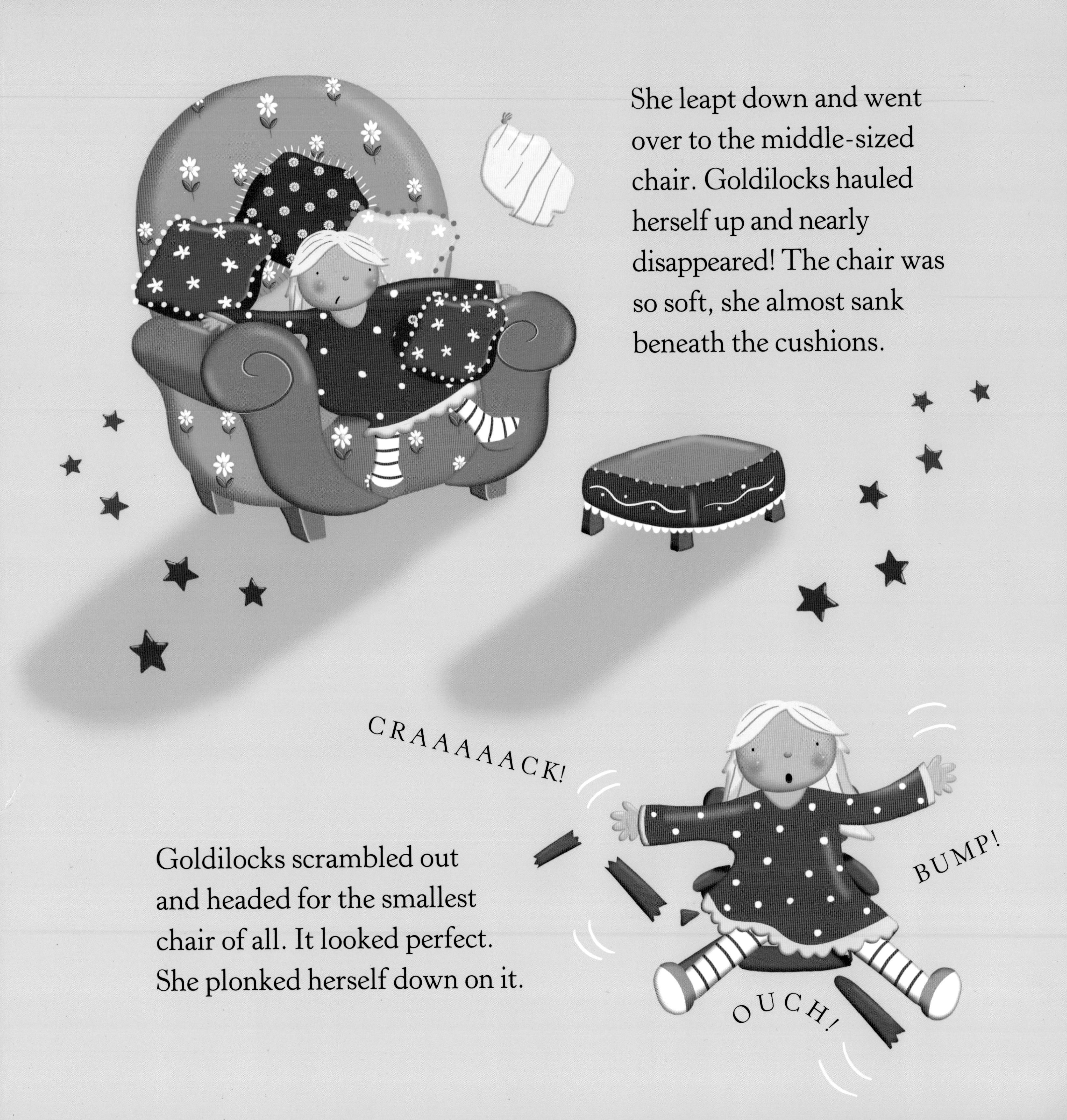

Goldilocks scrambled out and headed for the smallest chair of all. It looked perfect. She plonked herself down on it.

Suddenly, Goldilocks felt very tired. She spotted some stairs in the corner of the room and went over to them.

At the top of the stairs she found a bedroom with three beds. Goldilocks tested the largest.

"Ouch! Too hard!" she cried.

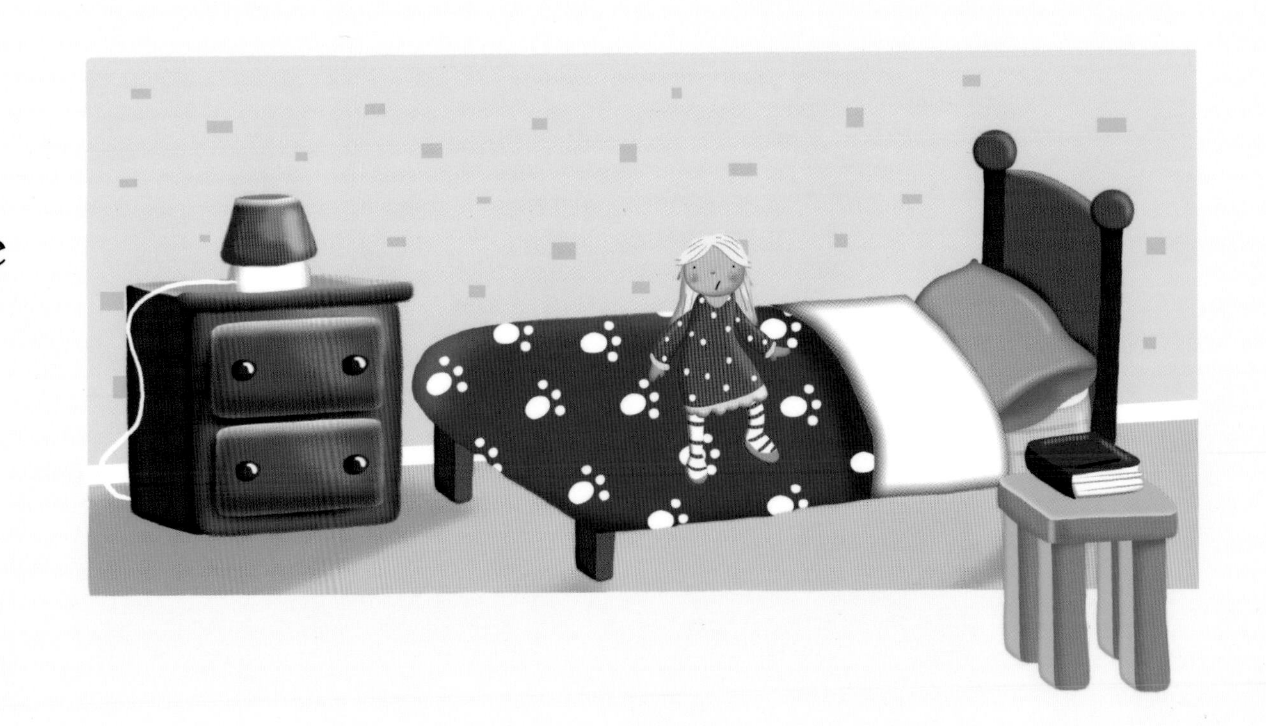

She jumped on to the middle-sized bed.

"Ooof! Too soft!" she groaned.

The smallest bed stood under the window. Goldilocks lay down on it. Aaah! Perfect! In a second, she was fast asleep.

While Goldilocks slept, the three bears came back from their walk.

"Someone's been eating my porridge!" Father bear growled.
"Someone's been eating my porridge!" said Mother Bear.
"Someone's been eating my porridge," cried Baby Bear, "and they've eaten it all up!"

Father Bear strode into the living room. "Someone's been sitting in my chair!" he muttered. "Someone's been sitting in my chair, too," said Mother Bear. "Oooh!" wailed Baby Bear, "someone's been sitting in my chair – and it's all broken!"